Baby Bear,
Baby Bear,
What Do You See?

By Bill Martin Jr
Pictures by Eric Carle

PUFFIN

Baby Bear,
Baby Bear,
what do you see?

I see a red fox
slipping by me.

Red Fox,
Red Fox,
what do you see?

I see a flying squirrel
gliding by me.

Flying Squirrel,
Flying Squirrel,
what do you see?

I see a mountain goat
climbing near me.

Mountain Goat,
Mountain Goat,
what do you see?

I see a blue heron
flying by me.

Blue Heron,
Blue Heron,
what do you see?

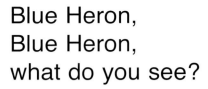

I see a prairie dog
digging by me.

Prairie Dog,
Prairie Dog,
what do you see?

I see a striped skunk
strutting by me.

Striped Skunk,
Striped Skunk,
what do you see?

I see a mule deer
running by me.

Mule Deer,
Mule Deer,
what do you see?

I see a rattlesnake
sliding by me.

Rattlesnake,
Rattlesnake,
what do you see?

I see a screech owl
hooting at me.

Screech Owl,
Screech Owl,
what do you see?

I see a mama bear
looking at me.

Mama Bear,
Mama Bear,
what do you see?

I see . . .

a red fox,

a flying squirrel,

a prairie dog,

a striped skunk,

a screech owl and . . .

a mountain goat,   a blue heron,

a mule deer,   a rattlesnake,

**my baby bear
looking at me –
that's what I see!**